DARPA

CATACLYSM

Vol. III

MANUEL PELAEZ

DARPA
CATACLYSM

MANUEL PELAEZ

Darpa Cataclysm by Manuel Pelaez

ISBN 978-1-952027-94-9 (Paperback)
ISBN 978-1-952027-95-6 (Hardback)

This book is written to provide information and motivation to readers. Its purpose is not to render any type of psychological, legal, or professional advice of any kind. The content is the sole opinion and expression of the author, and not necessarily that of the publisher.

Printed in the United States of America.

New Leaf Media, LLC
175 S. 3rd Street, Suite 200
Columbus, OH 43215
www.thenewleafmedia.com

Chapter 1

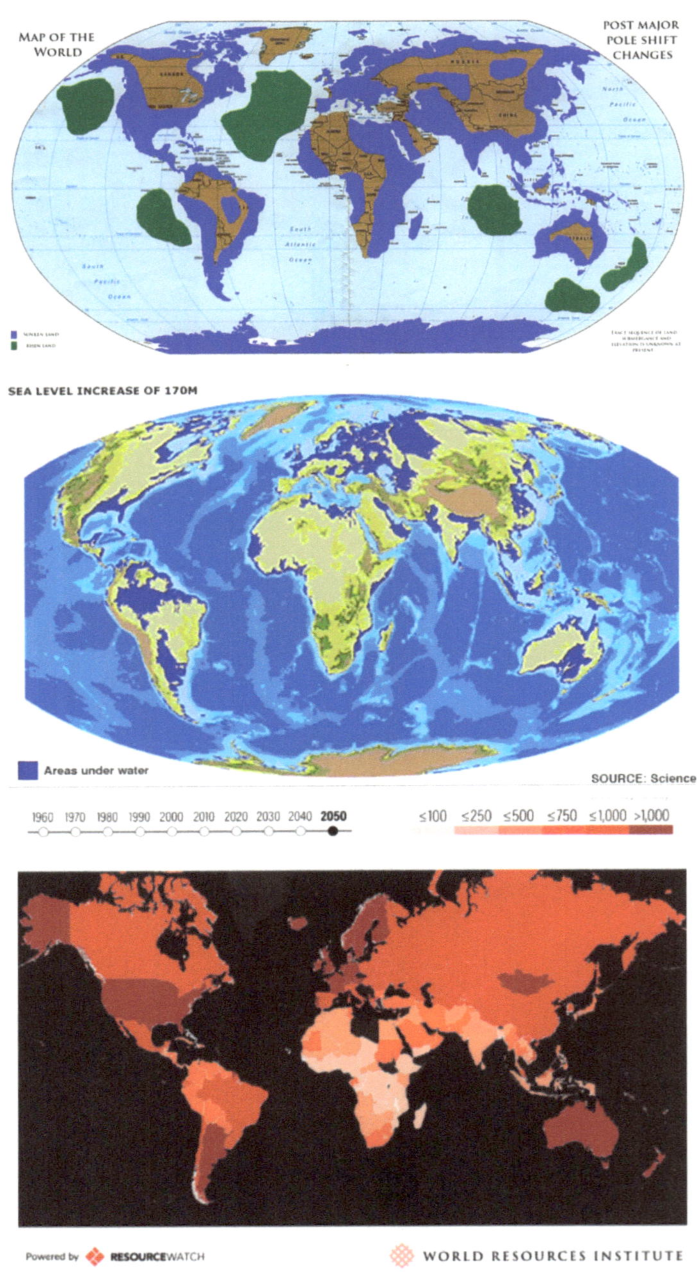

The ignorance of mankind continued especially with its world leaders, fossil fuels, greenhouse gases, deforestation, ocean acidification, climate change, global warming, bio-genic pollution, human induced pollution, techno centrism, chemical effluents, transport, unplanned construction, secondary pollutants, defective agricultural, policies, the population explosion, arbitrary land-use policies. This ignorance is effecting many areas worldwide, Greenland's glaciers, Alaska's glaciers and forestry, Siberia's Forestry, Canada's glaciers and forestry, the entire Arctic Circle, South America's Rainforest, many parts of the United States. Glaciers melting, fires ranging out of control, the deterioration was noticeable everywhere, droughts, fast floods. Bomb cyclones causing (winter storms, tornadic thunderstorms, damaging winds, severe blizzards, even flooding). Tropical cyclones (dumping trillions of gallons of rainwater) in a short amount of time. The following charts are projections on how our precious Earth will look like in 2050, many parts of habitable land will be lost to our oceans. Even worse is Earth's heat index for 2050, the other charts are even worse after 2050.

CHAPTER 2

The ignorance of world leaders persisted, Whit and Shu (the special kids of the late Zon), were constantly being interrogated by the top military command brass. They were ordered to go and gather the other special ones that possess their special abilities to communicate with land animals and sea creatures. Whit and Shu truly tried their very best to warn the world leaders, keeping their promise to the Massive Space Energy Sphere before they left our atmosphere and returned home. Whit and Shu both felt something wrong a distrust among the top military command brass. Before getting started in gathering the other special ones located in different regions around the world. A passenger plane will be waiting for them in the morning to board, (a military escort wasn't necessary because they were not considered a national security risks). Even with that said a detailed light security detail was in place mostly in front of where they were residing.

Chapter 3

Director Jones from CIA in the very beginning gave extremely secretive instructions on what certain individuals should do in case of a life and death scenario (for which no one knows about). These individuals will receive a very complex encrypted message (a series of numbers and letters). The following individuals were instructed to drop everything they are doing at the moment, and just take off not telling absolutely no one, to a nearby abandoned airfield. They were carefully instructed to not take anything including watches, belts, no electronic devices, especially cellphones, jewelry, bags, etc. The following individuals receive the encrypted message, Whit, Shu, The small team of engineering scientists, Marcus (Izem), Julie (the neurologist), their daughters are included. The moment each of them receive the encrypted message, there is no hesitation to follow very strict instructions. When Whit and Shu receive the encrypted message they quickly left through the back window of where they are residing, the light security detail didn't even notice. Whit uses his telepathic abilities to summon two wild horses to transport them to the site. When each engineer scientist receives the encrypted message, they do exactly what they were instructed to do. Each of them left everything behind (late afternoon), each of them got into one of the scientists vehicle and left. Each of them knew that any hesitation can cause them their lives and place the future of DARPA in great jeopardy. When Marcus (Izem) and Julie receive the encrypted message at first they were shocked but didn't hesitate to follow the strict instructions. Leaving everything behind and taking their twin daughters in their vehicle as they head towards the abandoned airfield. As everyone arrives to the abandoned airfield Director Jones is already at the site waiting for them. Director Jones tells everyone I know you all have a lot of questions but right now we must all get inside the small plane (a twin propeller MERLÍN lll, capable of reaching 2239 miles) and as we flee, we must come up with a plan where we can hide from DARPA which will be almost impossible. Once we are airborne I can tell you what's happening, (Director Jones is a pilot and has kept flying a hobby). Everyone gets inside the small plane and they take off, leaving everything behind.

CHAPTER 4

Once airborne Director Jones tells Marcus (Izem), Whit and Shu to help them come up with solutions on where they can hide from DARPA, (Director Jones has a complete map of Virginia Beach in Virginia, Virginia, and West Virginia in rural areas marked exactly where the manual cannons are located inside a waterproof bag with zip lock). Marcus (Izem) and Whit look at each other as they know exactly where DARPA cannot get to them. Marcus (Izem) goes on to say we can hide among (donkere here) the dark lord's and their forbidden underground cities. Marcus (Izem) continues to say they will accept us after I explain to them what exactly is happening. Director Jones sets a course towards Africa, but adds to the urgency of what they are facing. Director Jones continues to say, the odds are stacked up against us, it will be a miracle if we get to Africa. Director Jones says, for starters if we don't have some kind of barrier in the skies to protect us from the autonomous supersonic drones and spider drones, not to mention the autonomous underwater drones, we don't stand a chance. Director Jones continues to say, we don't have enough fuel to make it to Africa, it's a good possibility we need to make a very difficult crash landing somewhere in the coast of Africa. Director Jones continues to say, how in the world we are going to swim towards the coast from far away in open waters. Whit is the first one to demonstrate the sheer telepathic powers he truly possesses. Director Jones promises everyone that he will get into details of what is going on inside DARPA headquarters when the more pressing matters are solved. Marcus (Izem) tells everyone to seat in front of the plane to allow Whit to use his telepathic abilities to give them a fighting chance of reaching the coast of Africa.

CHAPTER 5

As if everyone is dreaming the skies appear to turn black, when everyone takes a closer look it's the formation of hundreds of thousands of birds. A combination of great reed warblers, the red backed shrikes, common cranes, bar-headed gooses, and ruppell griffon vultures. Everyone inside the plane is in complete shock of what they are witnessing. Director Jones says, this will keep away the autonomous supersonic drones and spider drones, but this is only part of our problems. Director Jones continues to say, we are currently cruising at 26,000 feet and will run out of fuel approximately after reaching 2,239 miles. The destination where we are headed is the coast of Africa which is 3,903 miles away. We will definitely run out of fuel before approximately 1,664 miles short of our destination. Since we are at 26,000 feet in attitude, when both propeller engines stop, the drag ratio is 10-1, around 10 miles forward we will lose 1 mile in attitude, meaning we will glide for at least 50 miles more before attempting an emergency landing in open waters (referred to as ditching). At that point, we only have 90 seconds to five minutes to exit the plane before it completely sinks to the bottom. Things will get a lot worse from there, we must try our best to avoid inflatable rafts and life vest.

Chapter 6

These open waters are shark infested waters, we won't last the night unless a miracle happens. Marcus (Izem) tells Director Jones that's why we have Shu, let her abilities come through for us when the time comes. Director Jones tells Marcus (Izem), you see that black box by the entrance of the bathroom, it contains nine adult sizes and two teenager sizes, and they have name tags on them. I have two extra adult sizes just in case if Whit and Shu want to change, but I know they already have amazing technological suits on, it is crucial not to trust DARPA at this point just in case of hidden tracking devices. Director Jones continues to say, I've been preparing for this type of emergency. Marcus (Izem) tells Director Jones, I'll take charge of this right away, and walks towards everyone to ask them to begin getting changed into the wetsuits.

CHAPTER 7

Marcus (Izem) opens the black box and starts handing out each wetsuit to each individual, requesting them to hurry because we don't have much time. One by one they change into the wetsuits, and complete this task knowing the greater danger ahead. Whit and Shu don't need to change they are equipped with special suits that have many features on them, but they both know what Director Jones said makes a lot of sense so they both change as well. When it's Director Jones turn he simply puts the plane on autopilot and changes into his wetsuit inside the bathroom. Afterwards, Director Jones returns to the cockpit and tells everyone that shortly they will run out of fuel and start gliding slowly downwards. We will be gliding for at least 50 miles more until I attempt to land the plane at sea. When we run out of fuel everyone secure your sit belts tightly and bend downwards towards your knees. Hopefully, the impact won't tear the plane apart, this isn't going to be easy. After the landing at sea is when we need another miracle before the sharks come. After being in flight for some time, Director Jones tells everyone we have just ran out of fuel, now we will begin the gliding process. We are currently at 26,000 feet, it's a 10-1 drag ratio, for every 10 miles forward we lose 1 mile in attitude.

Chapter 8

The landing itself, the speed, water state, and the aircraft pitch or roll can all have a massive effect. We need preferably flat water and a well-controlled descent (or ditching) to have a positive outcome. The cabin air valves which will be underwater will be closed by the pilot with a switch in the cockpit, otherwise, the water will come in the aircraft. The plane will stay afloat long enough for everyone to get out through the emergency exit. We need at all cost to avoid life jackets and inflatable life rafts, this is crucial because DARPA will detect us and it's game over. We must become almost invisible and well camouflaged to avoid the entire DARPA apparatus. We need many miracles to happen first the emergency landing in open waters (calm waters). Second, find a way of getting to shore without being devoured by sharks, and drowning. Third, how are we going through the autonomous underwater drones which are patrolling our oceans as we get closer to shore? Forth, how are we going to travel on land to our destination, without being detected by DARPA. Marcus (Izem) tells Director Jones to just calm down and focus on the landing out at sea safely. Whit and Shu will take it from there with their amazing abilities, solving all the miracles we desperately need. Director Jones is trying his best to slowdown the plane as much as possible, keeping landing gear stowed (stowed position not in use). Keep the nose up slightly, but not so much that the aircraft slams down roughly on contact. Keep the wings level to prevent one from being clipped by a wave, causing the aircraft to go into a spin or break apart. In a water landing, an aircraft's aluminum skin can bend and dent on impact. A water landing has much better results than a water crash which could cause cartwheeling, flipping, or break apart. Here we go, ten, nine, eight, seven, six, five, four, three, two, one, impact, and the plane slides on its belly through the ocean everything is happening so fast. As if in a nightmarish dream but with luck on their side the waters are calm, the plane slides on top of the water on its belly in open waters. Everyone appears to be alive, the impact itself was rough but the plane appears to be intact. Now, all the attention is getting out as fast as possible, a quick check to make sure everyone is alive.

CHAPTER 9

The emergency exit is open, one by one they exit the plane, Shu uses her telepathic abilities to summon a pod of short-fin pilot whales (Globicephala Macrorhynchus). In no time at all a pod of 40 short-fin pilot whales show up, Shu ensures the group that they will not be harmed. One by one each one mount themselves on the back of a giant short-fin pilot whale, holding on to their dorsal fin. Each one is on an individual short-fin pilot whale holding on tightly to their dorsal fin on their backs. At a distance they can see the plane sink disappearing to the ocean's bottom. Now, their journey begins towards the coast, Shu tells Director Jones that as they get closer to within the protection zone of patrolling autonomous underwater drones. Shu ensures the group as they get closer to within the protection zone, pods of southern right whales (Eubalaena Australis) and humpback whales (Megaptera Novaeangliae) will create a path for us to pass. The giant whales will bump the autonomous underwater drones if necessary, but usually what happens is that the autonomous underwater drones avoid contact. Director Jones knows the clock is ticking for them, Whit continues using his telepathic abilities to continue hundreds of thousands of birds above them. The autonomous supersonic drones and spider drones are equally deadly, the entire DARPA security apparatus is too powerful to take on. By using nature itself the creatures that inhabit Earth, it makes the group almost invisible and blend in with natural elements. Director Jones had food and water on board the plane so the group is fine for now, but afterwards whenever they reach shore they really need to get creative to continue surviving. The pod of short-fin pilot whales (Globicephala Macrorhynchus) are a force in the seas, they are extremely powerful and can travel through the seas with great ease. Measuring up to 20 feet in length and weighing in at 6,600 lbs, traveling at 20 mph it will take the group around 11 hours to reach their destination and make it to shore. After traveling for many hours and entering the protection zone the larger whales set a path for them clearing the way of being detected by the autonomous underwater drones. Whit is using his telepathic abilities for an air shield above the skies to clear the path for them above and avoid being detected by the autonomous supersonic drones and spider drones.

Chapter 10

Whit will now use his telepathic reach to summon a herd of African elephants to help them on land reach their destination to the dark lords (donkere here) forbidden underground cities. With the help of the larger whales (southern right whales and humpback whales) the group finally makes it past the protection zone, the pod of 40 short-fin pilot whales (Globicephala Macrorhynchus) takes them right up to the shores. The group quickly swim to land where the elephants one by one lower themselves so each of them can ride on top of an individual elephant. On top of the skies are hundreds of thousands of birds providing an air shield so they won't be detected by the autonomous supersonic drones and spider drones. The herd of elephants shall travel through savannas, mountains, deserts, forest habitats, and grasslands, until they reach their unknown destination. The group needs to rest, and the herd of elephants shall provide them with fruits and vegetables that are commonly known in the regions. Director Jones begins telling the others what exactly has happened to trigger all these things in motion. Director Jones begins by saying, DARPA itself is being taken over by a very powerful group working in the shadows, this group is known as the (inner circle). I needed to act fast before DARPA goes dark, because after that point we will be labeled (suspicious fugitives), which carries a death sentence. There was absolutely no time to think only send out an encrypted message which all of you understand. Time is against us, we don't have the luxury of waiting because things are about to get much worse. Thank God, for your special abilities and also having the knowhow of where we can hide from DARPA. Hopefully, our journey doesn't get us detected by DARPA, and we're able to reach the forbidden underground cities. Our lives depends on it, the cover we have above helps out a lot and the way we are traveling also helps out, but we need to hide from DARPA fast before the transformation into darkness fully happens. We shall rest for periods of time and eat on the go, but it's extremely important to hide from DARPA's reach as soon as possible.

CHAPTER 11

Meanwhile, back when the (Secret Order) was having their meeting at the sacred tombs located in Africa. Terrence (Soldaat), quickly knew something was terribly wrong when there was absolutely no lights anywhere, even from a distance the cities were dark. At that point Terrence (Soldaat) knew that he and the six leaders needed to go somewhere safe. Terrence (Soldaat) just like his brother Marcus (Izem) knew of such a place. Terrence (Soldaat) and his brother Marcus (Izem) since they were smaller knew the stories of a forbidden underground cities and its people called the dark lord's. Terrence (Soldaat) remembers taking his brother Marcus (Izem) to the elder tribal leader Zon. Terrence (Soldaat) has an idea where the forbidden underground cities are but doesn't know exactly. He quickly tells the others let's go to this unknown location and stay hidden in the mountains, we shall have a post of each of us looking out for any signs of my brother Marcus (Izem). The minute any of you spot him call out to me using your small animal horn around your necks. Terrence (Soldaat) makes it perfectly clear that he alone shall reach out to his brother Marcus (Izem). They begin their journey traveling by horseback to the site, at the sacred tombs location they leave an arsenal of weaponry whenever they desperately need it one day. They are armed but hidden in small caves underground they have explosives, ropes, more firepower, waterproof bags, ropes, canned foods, water, if needed one day. Both Terrence (Soldaat) and Marcus (Izem) since they were small kids growing up they knew that the forbidden underground cities and the dark lord's, were the safest place in the entire world to hide from anything, and Terrence (Soldaat) is banking on this idea that his brother Marcus (Izem) will also seek this place to hide. Terrence (Soldaat) knows his options are limited to what is happening on our world and requires quick rational thinking for their survival. Terrence (Soldaat) tells the other six leaders of the group to sound the animal small horn the minute they witness anything unusual, something bizarre, and irregular. The minute I hear the sound of the small horn I will travel to your post by horse to engage and hopefully find my brother Marcus (Izem). Terrence (Soldaat) and the six leaders arrive at the unknown location traveling by horse and walking the rest of the way they carefully take their post. The two brothers have not seen each other since they were teenagers and were separated by tragic events occurring in their country, Marcus (Izem) always assumed that his brother Terrence (Soldaat) that presumed dead. If they see each other again Marcus (Izem) will be in total shock as if he is seeing a ghost, Terrence (Soldaat) knows exactly what to say to him for him to know it's him in the flesh. Since teenagers Terrence (Soldaat) always called his younger brother (Jonger Broer Izem) in African translation, which means (younger brother Izem) in english. After a considerable amount of time passes, one of the leader spotter sees a massive dark cloud above, the leader spotter notices that it's hundreds of thousands of birds. The leader spotter quickly sounds the small horn echoing in a distance, signaling to Terrence (Soldaat) exactly as he was instructed. Without any hesitation Terrence (Soldaat) takes off by horseback towards the sound, when arriving on site where the spotter is located he sees the massive dark clouds of birds. Terrence (Soldaat) tells the spotter to stay there while he goes off to investigate this strange phenomenon. As Terrence (Soldaat) gets closer to the massive dark clouds above he realizes that it's hundreds of thousands of birds and he can also hear the stumping of the large herd of elephants. He quickly can see the group carefully divided and riding on individual elephants. Terrence (Soldaat) shouts out (Jonger Broer Izem), suddenly Marcus (Izem) recognizes that voice. The elephant Marcus (Izem) is riding on bows down to allow him to get off, and Terrence (Soldaat) gets off his horse as well. The two brothers embrace each other with tears running down their faces, Marcus (Izem) and Terrence (Soldaat) are completely speechless, and they have so much to talk about. For the time being they must set everything aside and deal with the realities facing them all its life and death. They all gather together hidden in the surroundings this includes both groups, they know they have little time to hide before DARPA's transformation into darkness.

CHAPTER 12

Marcus (Izem) begins to talk to both groups this includes Director Jones, the team of engineering scientists which are four in total, Whit, Shu, Marcus's wife Julie, their twin daughters, Terrence (Soldaat), the six regional leaders (which are part of the Secret Order). Marcus (Izem) carefully explains to everyone we are all about to enter sacred grounds, the dark lords (donkere here) first need to accept our group. No one knows how long we will be living among them, I'm telling everyone know they hardly speak, we will be completely a part of their traditions and cultures. We will be separated (men and women) in work assignments in groups, we will dress like them, they have a special clay they put on their skins, they grow their own food, everything we need to stay hidden and alive. Remember, the golden rule absolutely no arguing, no rebellious behavior, they will cover our eyes before entering their forbidden underground cities, Marcus (Izem) lived among the dark lords and their forbidden underground cities. Whit says, I will explain to them what is happening on our world, even though, they have nothing to do with our civilization they know that if things get any worse it will affect them also. We need once inside the forbidden underground cities to come up with a strategy or concrete plan to salvage our world. Whit and Shu are next to address important developments, as things develop on our world, both myself and my sister are able to detect the formations of communications among the Earth species. We will know when it's best to mobilize our strategy or plan, DARPA has many capabilities and we need to be very patient and smart moving forward. Whit (known as the keeper to the dark lords, following his late father Zon), now, tells everyone to wait here as he goes and attempts to speak to the dark lords (donkere here). Whit, has been chosen by his late father Zon before he passed away to be the one sibling that is able to communicate with the dark lords. Whit, goes secretly to the location where he was taught from his late father Zon to make a series of bird and whistle noises, waiting patiently for the dark lords to reveal themselves. After time passes one dark lord appears like a ghost, the dark lords use a language that is a mixture of African and ancient African words.

Chapter 13

Whit, requests to talk to one of the leaders of the dark lords to explain everything. The dark lord tribal member quickly puts a cover over his head and carefully takes him inside the forbidden underground cities. Whit is embraced by one of the dark lord leaders, all the dark lords knew his legendary father Zon, Whit and his sister Shu are their spiritual children. The dark lords trust them both deeply, Whit starts to explain everything to the dark lord leader, exactly everything that's going on, the exact number of the group seeking shelter, who they are. The other dark lord tribal leaders are summoned to discuss everything, they gather among themselves. The dark lord leaders grant Whit and the others of the group permission to be with them inside the forbidden underground cities. Some dark lord tribal members cover up Whit head again taking more covers for the group and carefully take Whit outside again. Whit quickly goes to gather the rest of the group while the dark lords wait hidden. Whit gathers the group and everyone quickly follows Whit to the location, the dark lords are very mysterious and like ghosts they appear putting on covers over the head of each member of the group. The dark lords carefully takes the group inside the forbidden underground cities. Once inside the group is embraced by the dark lord tribal leaders, they especially hug Marcus (Izem) and Terrence (Soldaat). Introductions are in order and one by one they introduce themselves. The dark lord tribal leaders say in their language now you are all part of our family. Back at DARPA headquarters the series of events are horrific, slowly DARPA and the other superpower nations version of their own advanced technologies in robotic engineering, the leadership is changing to a much darker transition.

CHAPTER 14

In secret a powerful organization known as the (Inner Circle) is taking over the leadership command. This secretive powerful organization is composed of the highest military command with the wealthiest individuals. The (Inner Circle) raise has many followers within the military and they see the advanced technologies of DARPA is the ultimate power to worldwide domination. The events that are about to take place are gruesome and very graphic, these events will be broken down in timelines, this is to fully understand what happens when mankind hungers for the ultimate power. The very first thing on the agenda for the (Inner Circle) is creating the ultimate power weapon (zero point energy). The powerful leaders of the (Inner Circle) knew that they desperately needed a weapon to somehow fight against the Massive Energy Sphere. The (Inner Circle) knows that the Massive Energy Sphere has technologies that are unmatched to anything on Earth. They also are aware that the entire energy grids on Earth will be useless once they arrive in our solar system. They know that the scientists need to somehow make a manual cannon to launch such a weapon. This type of weapon doesn't need any energy to function, so whenever the entire energy grid of our world is completely shutoff they have a secret weapon to fight back.

Chapter 15

Now, let's begin with the scientific advancements that made this weapon possible, breaking down the impossibilities and dangers of creating a zero point energy weapon. Physicists have calculated the zero-point radiation of the vacuum to be an order of magnitude greater than nuclear energy, with one teacup containing enough energy to boil all the world's oceans. The zero-point energy cannot be harnessed in the traditional sense, the idea of zero-point energy is that there is a finite, minimum amount of motion (more accurately, kinetic energy). One should not take this (vacuum energy) too literally, because the (free-field theory) is just a mathematical tool to help us understand (interacting theory). These vacuum fluctuations may have effects, both subtle and gross, behavior of microscopic particles. Nobody knows how to exploit the zero-point energy in a macroscopic device that delivers sizable amounts of energy. Random quantum fluctuations of the electromagnetic (and other) force fields are everywhere in the vacuum. An "empty" vacuum is actually a seething cauldron of energy, even at absolute zero temperature (-273 Celsius). Predictions and experiments from physicists gave a very precise and unambiguous confirmation of the existence of the Casimir Force. It is within these breakthroughs that scientists and physicists have made great contributions towards the reality of a zero-point energy weapon. The zero-point energy weapon will use only drops of this overwhelming energy source and fired at enormous distances. DARPA's secret weapon is a modified M777A2 mobile Howitzer, this massive extended range cannon artillery weapon (ERCA) is designed to hit ranges beyond 80 kilometers. The Earth's atmosphere dissipates as you gain elevation 62 miles (100 kilometers) straight up. DARPA's secret weapon is completely manual and the plan is to launch the massive cannon a shell containing small amounts of zero-point energy directly at one of the massive quarter sphere when positioned around the Earth in orbit. Scientists and Physicists don't know what will happen with a blast of that magnitude, but it's DARPA's only defense against the Massive Space Sphere with origin and technologies are completely unknown to our world.

CHAPTER 16

The first thing that the (Inner Circle) after assuming absolute power, is form they own military with loyal followers. Each of these followers will give their lives to ultimate power on our world, the leadership within them extends worldwide and are ruthless. The first thing on the agenda is to release all the Earth's species that were inside the habitats of (UNI-WORLD) free. This entire process has a more cynical plan which will be revealed soon. One by one each habitat is emptied, let's begin with (ARCTIC-SPHERE), each species are released in their natural environments. Let's move on to (TROPIC-JUNGLES), each species are released in their natural environments. DARPA continues releasing the species with (THE-PLAINS), each species are released in their natural entertainment to increase their chances of survival. It is time consuming but this process is necessary for a greater cynical plan, they continue with (RIVER-BASINS). The special collars placed on the species while inside the habitat to control the species are removed, they continue with (WILDERNESS), these collars make it easy to track the species. Now, they carefully remove the deep sea creatures in the special exhibits like (INTO THE DARK) and (ENCOUNTERS), these rare species are placed back in their environments. We now arrive at the sea creatures in the underwater lagoon (SEA ODYSSEY), after some time passes by all the habitats and special exhibits are empty.

CHAPTER 17

The events that are about to take place from this point forward are very graphic and gruesome. A full list of names are written in documents in the hands of the top military leaders with are 100% loyal to the (Inner Circle). This horrific list contains the names of personal that were the previous leadership of DARPA, every name on that list will be executed. Secret executions will be taking place every single day, those who are not found on this list will be labeled (suspicious fugitives) which is clearly a death sentence. The nightmares begin, groups after groups of the previous DARPA command start being executed every single day. May God have mercy on them, these individuals are top government officials like Congressman Chris Whitman. Many other top officials are being executed, this reality is nothing short of a nightmare to what's coming next. One group after another are being executed, the individuals that are not found are the following, Director Jones, Whit, Shu, The team of engineering scientists which names are, Jon Tan Lan, Sam Andre Dame, Marcus Johnson (Izem), Tim Von Gleason, Ron Ben Ruckman, they are all labeled (suspicious fugitives), they will be hunted worldwide. It's a sad day for what's happening on our world, the executions are happening like clockwork. Now, we begin with even more horrific events that are about to take place. The Earth itself has deteriorated so much that many habitable regions are completely underwater, this has triggered DARPA calling what was (UNI-WORLD) and other parts that has the capability of housing hundreds of thousands of refugees.

Now, the new name is called (re-evacuation zones), making everyone believe it's safe where shelter is dry, food and water. It was all lies, once everyone was relocated to these (re-evacuation zones), the mighty DARPA security apparatus composed of an outside fencing was in fact an interconnected laser network system with high energy laser towers (HEL), carefully placed 1000 feet from each other. Absolutely no one stands a chance with this type of technologies, to make it even worse buffer zones were in place 50 to 75 feet from the perimeters. Even was then that are the giant super soldiers that stand about 8 to 7 feet in height patrolling the outside perimeters like giant guards. Absolutely anyone trying to escape are completely vaporized with some sophisticated lasers. In the skies above traveling at enormous speeds are autonomous supersonic drones, and spider drones that also move anywhere, both are equipped with lasers and missiles. This entire experience is a complete nightmare all we can do is pray and accept our new realities. DARPA and military personnel's extremely loyal to the (Inner Circle), started invading regions, rounding up people like cattle. Any rebellious acts, or resistance, were completely vaporized, people tried to fight back but how can anyone fight back with these autonomous robotic technologies. This was our realization now, every single day thousands of people will be placed in these (re-evacuation zones). Many people fled to the mountains and wilderness to live like animals, but DARPA and the military personnel's don't ever stop hunting them down. Even in the oceans DARPA has autonomous underwater drones, which are capable of spotting anyone even at night. People will look at each other saying with their eyes how long is this nightmare going to last. Inside the (re-evacuation zones), we were given food but like cattle and sheep, in big pots little bowls for each of us, we took baths in large groups exactly like zoo animals. All we can do is try to survive and prey in groups, we must stay strong and encourage each individual next to you not to give up. With that said, there were many deaths the weak, and sick, it seemed hopeless many times. We were separated by gender in groups, the children were housed separately and gender also. We had to clean up after our selves, make food for the others, clean clothes, the children had teachers to somehow be occupied. The DARPA security apparatus meant business any disobedience were vaporized right in front of everyone like a warning. No one dared to ask any questions about anything, those giant super soldiers looked scary as hell. What no one knew not even the (Inner Circle) or its top loyal military command brass.

CHAPTER 18

When they released the species of Earth they were sending out a distress signals to the Massive Space Energy Sphere in various forms of communications. The following are the various forms of communication of our Earth species, very low frequencies, sound waves called (echolocation), weak electrical signals, audible sounds, infra-sounds, signature whistles. The Earth's species know that our planet is deteriorating badly and sooner or later they will be slaughtered in record numbers.

Chapter 19

What DARPA and the military top command didn't know is that the Massive Space Energy Sphere left behind on Earth hundreds of thousands of energy individual microscopic cerebrum molecules. The ability of the Massive Space Energy Sphere to respond from the farthest regions of space will be much faster. DARPA and the top military brass have no knowledge of the origin of communication the Massive Space Energy Sphere uses, and so many other unanswered questions. The Massive Space Energy Sphere ability to travel many times at warp speed is unbelievable, Earth's technologies is no match for this unknown intelligence. Meanwhile, inside the forbidden underground cities Whit and Shu can hear and feel the species of Earth distress signals. Whit and Shu tell the rest of the group including the dark lords, Director Jones begins designing a plan of attack to takeout the massive cannons with Terrence (Soldaat) and the six regional leaders of the (Secret Order).

Chapter 20

Terrence (Soldaat) and the six regional leaders decided that they will execute the plan of attack because they are better equipped to handle this crisis, there is no one better to lead then Terrence (Soldaat). Director Jones has knowledge of exactly where the massive manual cannons are located, he knows the entire compound. The individuals of the group gather seated in a circle on the dirt while Director Jones takes out the map that has marked exactly where the landing should be by sea, which is Virgina Beach Virginia, Virginia and exactly where in rural areas in West Virginia the manual cannons are located. This plan must include everyone's input using the abilities of Whit and Shu, the knowledge and knowhow of Director Jones of the compound, the courage of Terrence (Soldaat), and the six regional leaders. Whit explains to everyone that this plan will go into effect the minute they arrive meaning the (Massive Space Energy Sphere), DARPA and the Earth's military command will be limited once the entire energy grids shutoff. After carefully discussing among themselves for some time the plan is as follows. First, Terrence (Soldaat) and the six regional leaders will go to the underground sacred tombs located right here in Africa traveling by horseback. At this location the group will load up with weaponry and supplies needed for this mission, things like explosives, machine guns, plenty of rope, night vision gear if necessary, flares, waterproof bags, food, water. Next, Terrence (Soldaat) and the six regional leaders will go to the coast and board a sailboat which they know exactly where some boats are tied up in a fishing village. Whit, will have wild horses waiting for them when they are outside the forbidden underground cities. Whit, will also have a small colony of African bats (later on it will be revealed why), the bats will travel with them mostly hidden in the cabin. Once, Terrence (Soldaat) and the six regional leaders arrive in the coast of Maryland, Whit will have wild horses waiting for the group. Shu, will have a small pod of blue whales (Balaenoptera Músculus), to tow the sailboat across the seas. This journey is about 4200 miles and will take at least 24 hours, ropes are extremely important to carefully tie around the massive mammal. Director Jones, has carefully mapped out the compound where the manual cannons are located with precise building and military personnel spots drawn on a map and has it inside a waterproof bag with a zip lock. Keep in mind, this entire mission is only made possible because DARPA's entire security apparatus will be shutdown, including the giant super soldiers, autonomous supersonic drones, spider drones, high energy laser towers (HEL), and the interconnected laser network fence barriers. Director Jones, warns Terrence (Soldaat) and the six regional leaders that once DARPA is shutdown things will be chaotic everywhere. Director Jones, continues saying your group will definitely be entering a hostile environment, DARPA still has thousands of soldiers, the manual firepower will still work like machine guns, explosives, etc. DARPA can only control so much, the massive manual cannons need to be calibrated before firing at such a difficult target. This window of opportunity can take a couple of days, get your sleep and be rested because there is no time to waste, we are on a precise timeline. The entire group understands what is at stake the salvation of our world, everyone understands that Director Jones, Whit and Shu, are the future and new beginning for DARPA. Terrence (Soldaat) and the six regional leaders know that Marcus (Izem) is a father now his family needs him. During the group planning this life and death mission, Marcus (Izem) wanted to go badly, so did Director Jones, Whit and Shu also.

CHAPTER 21

Terrence (Soldaat) replied, each of you will serve a greater purpose your courage is noted, but there isn't no future for DARPA without each of you. Terrence (Soldaat) goes on saying, I and my men have been staring at death our entire lives and we will succeed because we don't stand alone, we have all the spirits from our warriors in battle. Soon, the entire world will know this day, and change our future forever on Earth. Terrence (Soldaat) explains that his group needs a diversion badly for the DARPA and military personnel to be distracted and fire in the opposite direction while he and his men attack on their blind spot to destroy the massive manual cannons. Whit, responds saying throw the flare where you need the distraction to occur, when we are able to be outside I will telepathically send the small colony of bats to fly above the flare sending high frequency chirps which are over 100,000 waves per second. Humans are limited to hearing 20 to 20,000 waves per second, the Massive Space Energy Sphere will know exactly the location to send an energy type image that will definitely catch the attention of the military soldiers and fire everything they have at this image giving your men the window they need.

Chapter 22

Meanwhile, while everyone was planning the mission inside the forbidden underground cities. From the farthest regions of space the Massive Space Energy Sphere received the distress signals from the other energy individual microscopic cerebrum molecules. It is completely unknown to any Earth technology how the Massive Space Energy Sphere is able to communicate at such far distances. The Massive Space Energy Sphere descends completely camouflaged turning black to blend into space. Traveling at many times warp speed, the following are the galaxies that the intelligence of Earth knows of. Spiral (Sombrero), Disk, Round, Cigar Shaped, Giant Elliptical, Irregular, Merging, Milky Way Solar System. The Massive Space Energy Sphere bypasses (JWST) James Webb Space Telescope, and the Hubble Space Telescope. The Massive Space Energy Sphere enters the Milky Way Solar System undetected. Positioning itself on the other side of Earth's moon, still camouflaged in complete darkness matching the background of outer space itself.

The Massive Space Energy Sphere suddenly opens up into four identical quarters, three of the identical quarters position themselves exactly around the Earth. Still completely camouflaged, the other quarter breaks up into waves similar to currents, into trillions of individual energy microscopic cerebrum molecules. The current waves travel through space penetrating Earth's defensive satellites which are equipped with lasers and the United States Space Force developed by (Defense Advanced Research Projects Agency) called (DARPA).

CHAPTER 23

The United States Space Force is equipped with advanced technologies to take microscopic samples, this is for research purposes to determine the origin of technology within the individual energy microscopic cerebrum molecules. In the future if physicists and scientists can determine this technology it can become a breakthrough. The rest of the trillions of individual energy microscopic cerebrum molecules completely camouflaged enter the Earth's atmosphere penetrating Earth's energy sources. Nuclear energies, electrical grids, surveillance data, including television, radios, all forms of communications. Soon afterwards, a warning is issued worldwide on every network, this is to land all aircraft, bring in military submarines, to avoid a massive catastrophe worldwide. Earth's nuclear capabilities were disabled before issuing the warning. The entire Earth goes dark, all energy is shutoff, the entire DARPA apparatus is down including, the giant super soldiers, autonomous supersonic drones, spider drones. All military naval fleets, tanks, infantry assets, including missile capabilities, are completely shut down. The moment this event takes place, Whit and Shu inside the forbidden underground cities tell Terrence (Soldaat), and the six regional leaders, it's time, Director Jones hands the waterproof bag with a detailed map of everything to Terrence (Soldaat) that is needed for this mission. Quickly the dark lords are informed and they cover up the heads of Terrence (Soldaat) and the six regional leaders to take them so they can begin their mission.

Chapter 24

The underground cities is a massive maze inside, the group is taken away by the dark lord's, and the others are placed with the rest of the dark lord's. Director Jones, Whit, Shu, the four engineering scientists, Marcus (Izem), Julie and their twin daughters, all know that when things are safe they can finally leave the forbidden underground cities. The dark lord's carefully take Terrence (Soldaat), and the six regional leaders outside and remove the cover from their heads. At a distance seven wild mustangs are awaiting them to start their journey for the salvation of our world. Terrence (Soldaat) and the six regional leaders mount themselves one by one individually on each wild mustang, and head out towards the underground sacred tombs to load up with weaponry and supplies, changing into camouflaged clothes to be almost invisible for this operation. pon arrival at the underground sacred tombs they quickly gather the weaponry needed for this mission, machine guns, explosives, infrared lenses, flares, especially plenty of rope, waterproof bags, snacks, canned foods, water, they also change into camouflaged clothing, boots, everything they need. They understand time is crucial as the DARPA and the military personnel will begin the calculations of the massive manual cannons. After loading up with everything they need they head off towards the fishing village where there are plenty of different types of boats to choose from. Once at the fishing village they spot the perfect sailboat tied up and board to inspect to see if it can take the long journey in front of them. Terrence (Soldaat) tells the others this one is perfect, and with that said he quickly spots a small colony of bats flying in their direction and entering the cabin. errence (Soldaat) also sees a small pod of blue whales (Balaenoptera Musculus), they are massive in size and can reach speeds of 50 kilometers per hour (31mph). Terrence (Soldaat) and some of the others quickly spring into action tying the rope on the sailboat and driving into the water to tie the rope around the massive blue whale (Balaenoptera Musculus). The massive blue whale is completely calm allowing Terrence (Soldaat) and the others to tie the rope around its wide body. The waters where the sailboat was tied up was deep but the group still pushed off using long paddles to be in deeper waters to make things easier for the massive blue whale (Balaenoptera Musculus). The journey begins early in the morning as the blue whale tows the sailboat it is accompanied by other blue whales, they will cross the ocean and it will take at least 24 hours. Terrence (Soldaat) and the six regional leaders will rest as much as they could because what awakes them isn't easy. Traveling across the Atlantic Ocean over 4200 miles can be challenging taking on many changes in weather patterns but the enormous strength of a pod of blue whales (Balaenoptera Musculus), is unmatched. During the duration of 24 hours Terrence (Soldaat) and the six regional leaders experience choppy seas, severe down pours of rainfall, extreme heat, high winds. Trying to rest whenever they can, eating can foods, they brought water, only focused on what's ahead.

CHAPTER 25

Arriving at the shores of Virginia Beach Virginia, the blue whale (Balaenoptera Musculus) takes them as close as possible to the shore at that point some of the six regional leaders drive into the ocean to release the rope tied around the massive whale. Afterwards, they swim back to the sailboat and the other blue whales bump the boat closer to shore, while everyone in the sailboat use long wooden paddles rowing themselves onto the shore. After getting off the sailboat with their waterproof bags, Terrence (Soldaat) spots seven wild mustangs waiting in the distance, its morning when they finally arrive. Terrence (Soldaat) and his men mount onto the wild mustangs one by one (the mustangs are wild but controlled telepathically by Whit). Terrence (Soldaat) and his men find an empty store that has saddles and blankets for the wild mustangs and the long ride ahead of them, afterwards, they quickly set off to West Virginia, and on the map it shows that DARPA headquarters is located somewhere in Arlington Virginia. It also clearly shows that the manual cannons are in a rural area in West Virginia, hidden away from populated areas. Terrence (Soldaat) and the six regional leaders will be traveling at least 50 mph and it will take 8 to 9 hours on horseback, the small colony of bats will be followIng them at a distance. The small colony of bats play a vital role later on, by the time they arrive at West Virginia it will be dark pitch black everywhere because Earth's energy grid is completely shut down. As Terrence (Soldaat) and the six regional leaders head out across Virginia mostly taking back roads and stay out of plain sight. The group quickly notices how deteriorated things are, the clashes between DARPA's security apparatus and populated areas. The buildings are broken up in many places due to explosions by lasers and missiles blast and riddled with bullet holes.

Chapter 26

Thousands of people that have escaped from the (re-evacuation zones) are running in every direction seeking shelter trying to flee to safer zones. This all started ever since Earth's energy grids were shutdown, DARPA and the military personnel try to maintain control but without the giant super soldiers, autonomous supersonic drones, spider drones, and especially the interconnected laser network barriers with (HEL) high energy laser towers. The military soldiers are outnumbered by the population in the (re-evacuation zones), occasionally, the military soldiers fire on groups escaping. There's dead bodies everywhere, in many places Terrence (Soldaat) and his men see groups of people sleeping around trash cans set on fire all trying to stay warm. There's vehicle's stranded everywhere nothing works, there is no lights anywhere, it is chaos everywhere. Terrence (Soldaat) and his men stop occasionally to check exactly where they are located on the map that Director Jones gave them. The hours passed by and Terrence (Soldaat) and his men are making progress. In West Virginia where the zero-point energy manual cannons are located in a empty field in rural areas, the calibration of the manual cannons are being done and soon they will be set to fire at a very difficult target on Earth's atmosphere. What Terrence (Soldaat) and the six regional leaders aren't aware of is that the (Inner Circle) will be in a special area close to the site to witness history in the making.

CHAPTER 27

The (Inner Circle) are an extremely powerful group composed of world leaders from superpower nations, top military brass, the wealthiest individuals on Earth, their only desire is to have the ultimate power across our world. The scientists and physicists have made calculations of what will happen if such an explosion occurs in space, but in reality it's only a calculation no one knows for sure. DARPA, the military, and the (Inner Circle), feel that for them to achieve the ultimate power they must show the Massive Space Energy Sphere that Earth isn't vulnerable and this will send a crystal clear message. After many hours of riding horseback Terrence (Soldaat) and his men arrive in West Virginia it's already nighttime, as they draw closer to the site where the massive manual cannons are located each of them carefully review the map using a lighter as light. They carefully find exactly where they are on the map, approaching as hidden as possible. The small colony of bats are following them at a distance, it seems as if time is moving slowly and tonight the salvation of our world slowly lies on Terrence (Soldaat) leadership. The night continues and things are about to get very intense, it's a good thing that Terrence (Soldaat) and the six regional leaders have been involved in life and death situations many times. The group arrives in stealth mode completely camouflaged they put on their infrared night vision gear. They quickly spot the patrols and formation of the military personnel guarding the massive manual cannons. Terrence (Soldaat) and his men know it's going to be a long night, but this mission must be done before the calibrations are complete and ready to fire. The group carefully get into place with their weapons, explosives, flares, etc. Without making any noise and positioning themselves to toss the flare so the small colony of bats spring into action, where what happens next is nothing short of miraculous. Terrence (Soldaat) himself tosses the flare at a distance, he throws the flare with accuracy, precisely where the diversion is needed. The minute Terrence (Soldaat) throws the flare and it lands glowing in the pitch black field in which they are located. Quickly, the small colony of bats fly around precisely on top of the glowing flare burning on the ground. The small colony of bats are making high frequency chirps which are over 100,000 waves per second, humans are limited to to hearing 20 to 20,000 waves per second. The small colony of bats are actually sending signals to the Massive Space Energy Sphere, transmitting these high frequency waves the Massive Space Energy Sphere can precisely zoom in on their location.

CHAPTER 28

The following events are extremely gruesome and graphic they take place in a series of events which trigger horrific outcomes. Suddenly, in that pitch black field where a small flare burns glowing, a massive shaped energy image appears out of nowhere. This energy image is about 8 feet tall and 4 feet wide, glowing continuously in a golden type color. Absolutely everyone in that pitch black field is completely in shock of what they are witnessing. In one moment, without any thought the military soldiers that are posted around the massive zero-point manual cannons and the others in the surroundings start firing a mirage of bullets, throwing grenades. All in the direction of the energy image that's illuminating continuously in a golden color. The calibrations are complete and ready to fire the massive zero-point energy cannons, in this chaotic moment where the night is lighten up by gunfire and explosions. errence (Soldaat) and the six regional leaders secretly attack on military soldiers blindside, coming in by the back while they are firing nonstop at the energy image. -Terrence (Soldaat) and his men know that disabling the massive zero-point energy cannons will be almost impossible. The following event will go down in human history as the greatest tragedy ever on Earth. Terrence (Soldaat) and the six regional leaders decide to throw explosives at the zero-point energy cannons to completely destroy them instead of other impossible options.

(KABOOM!!!!), almost colorless and shapeless"a stupendous burst of light"a light not of this world "a ghastly pulsating radiance"the night turned day"green, pink, red, scarlet, purple, ethereal purple, violet, gold, yellow, yellow-white, white, multicolored all of the above. mushroom cloud"a think parasol"supra mundane"quivering"convulsively. Many times more powerful than the atomic bomb dropped in Hiroshima and Nagasaki. In one instant, Terrence (Soldaat), the six regional leaders, the (Inner Circle), the military top brass loyalists, the entire military personnel, and hundreds of thousands of people, are completely wiped out of existence. The minute this horrific event happens, inside the forbidden underground cities. Whit and Shu, can feel and hear the overwhelming pain of this catastrophic event.

CHAPTER 29

The minute Whit and Shu tell everyone inside the forbidden underground cities that something horrible has happened explaining of a untold amount of deaths. Marcus (Izem), yells out (BROER) in African, which means brother in english, with tears running down his face he drops down to his knees. The pain is too much to bare for Marcus (Izem), his wife Julie and his twin daughters try to all hug him and comfort him. There is total silence inside the forbidden underground cities, everyone can feel the overwhelming pain from Marcus's (Izem) heart. There is great sorrow everywhere, but it took a catastrophic event of unprecedented magnitude to lay down the foundation for a new beginning. It will take years of investigations to pinpoint exactly what happened on this day, and for the radiation to clear.

Chapter 30

One thing is for certain that a bronze plaque with the names of the departed shall be placed whenever DARPA rises again with a new leadership that will bring harmony to our world for humans and it's species to live together in peace. May the names of Terrence (Soldaat) and the six regional leaders once known as the (Secret Order) a terrorist organization, go down in history as heroes having unbelievable courage to fulfill the salvation of our world. May this tragic day teach the human race that if we didn't learn anything from World War One, or World War Two, this event shall mark the end of all future conflicts. May this day mark the new beginning of DARPA with Director Jones, Whit, Shu, (known as the special ones), and the engineering scientists named, Jon Tan Lan, Sam Andre Dame, Marcus Johnson, Tim Von Gleason, Ron Ben Ruckman. After years of investigations from different government agencies which includes the Nuclear Emergency Support Team (NEST), the Centers for Disease Control (CDC), Department of Homeland Security (DHA), Federal Emergency Management Agency (FEMA), and other top secret agencies, deploying many personnel in hazmat suits it will be known what series of events took place on this tragic day, other countries shall join this investigation in a joint corporation. The Massive Space Energy Sphere departure from Earth's atmosphere came after DARPA underwent a complete transition of leadership led by Director Jones and the team of engineering scientists, with the special ones (Whit and Shu) by his side, Marcus (Izem) remained retired, Earth's energy grids were restored as investigations persisted but without nuclear capabilities.